It's Raining TACOS!

by
PARRY GRIPP

Illustrated by
PETER EMMERICH

HARPER
An Imprint of HarperCollinsPublishers

It's my birthday!
It's going to be great!
Birthday, with pizza and cake.
All my friends will come celebrate.
Yay! It's my birthday!

For my birthday,
I've got a new pet.
A doggy!
Oh, she is the best!
The biggest, fluffiest pooch
that I've met.
A dog for my birthday!

It's my party! Outside in the sun,
We play games, we jump, and we run!
Prizes and fun for everyone,

What a great party!

Oh no! No, no-no-no-no-**no**,
Doggy, what did you do—ooh?

Oh no! No, no-no-no-no-**no**!
Not the pepperoni too—ooh?

Oh, it's my birthday,
what can I do?

There's cake and "Happy birthday to you!"
Do birthday wishes really come true?
I'll make a wish for my birthday!

I blow out the candles. What is that sound?
Thump! Thunk! On the roof really loud!
"Look outside! What's that on the ground?"

It's raining
TACOS!

It's raining tacos,
from out of the sky.

TACOS,
no need to ask why.

Just open your mouth
and close your eyes.

It's raining tacos!

It's raining tacos, out in the street.
Tacos, all you can eat.
Lettuce and shells, cheese and meat.
It's raining tacos!

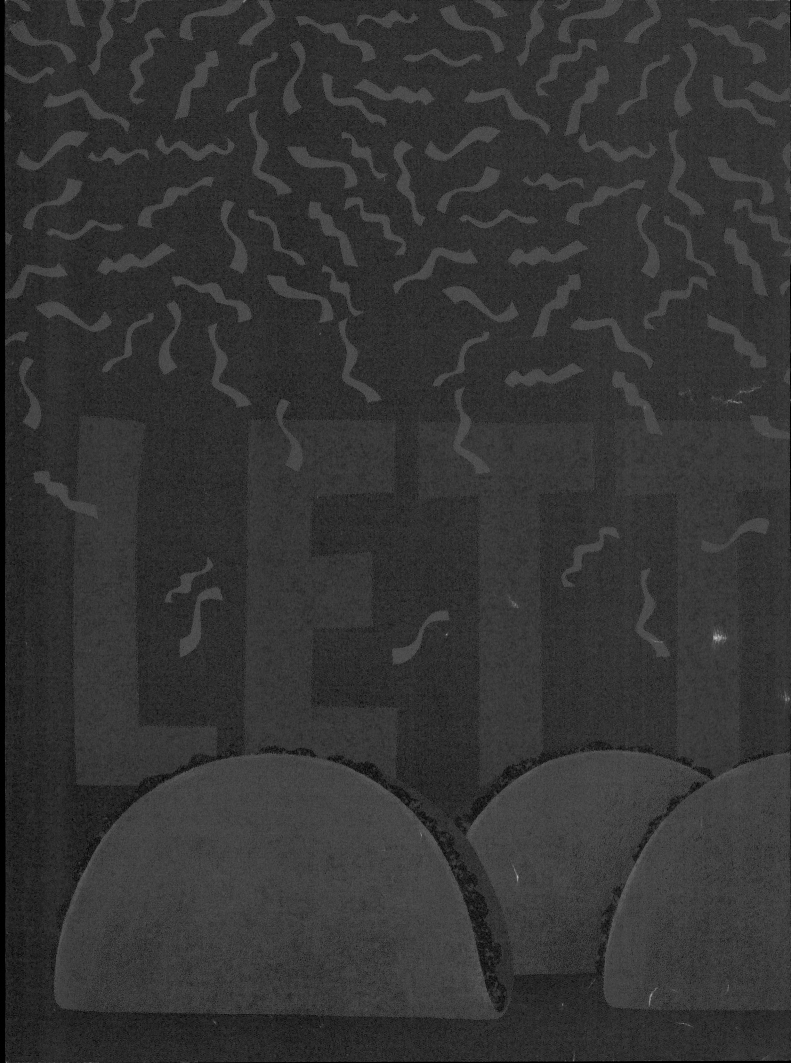

SHELL,

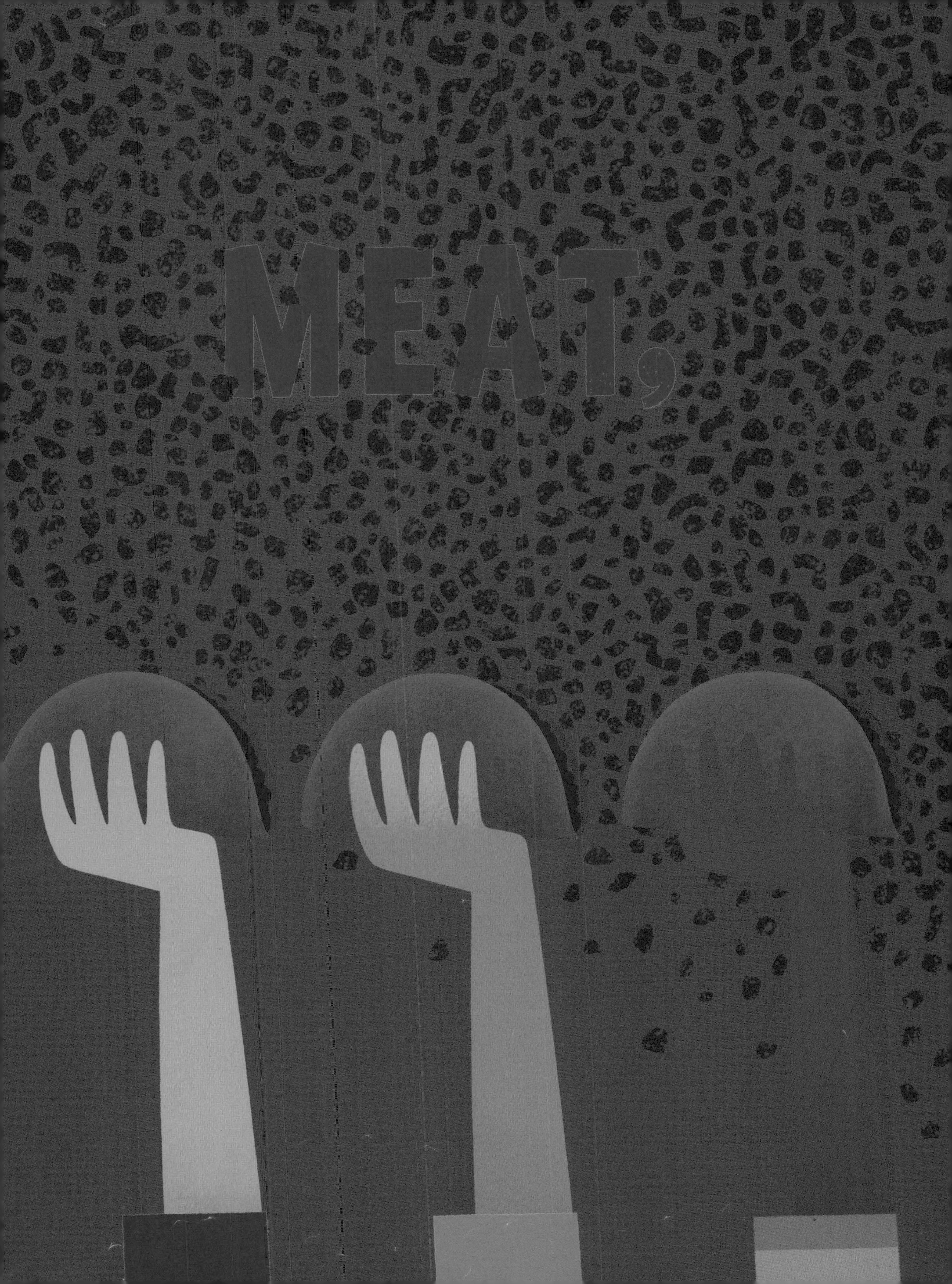
MEAT,

It's raining tacos!

Yes, it's my birthday! It turned out great!
Birthday, we ate tacos and cake.
With my friends and my dog to help celebrate.

YAY!
It's my
birthday!

For Aylene, whose love writes
the melodies of my songs, and whose
words wrote much of this book.

—P.G.

For my mother and father,
who gave me constant love and support.

—P.E.

It's Raining Tacos!
Text copyright © 2021 by Parry Gripp
Illustrations copyright © 2021 by Peter Emmerich
All rights reserved. Manufactured in Italy.

Library of Congress Control Number: 2020938935
ISBN 978-0-06-300647-8

The artist used Photoshop to create the digital illustrations for this book.
Typography by Carla Weise
21 22 23 24 25 RTLO 10 9 8 7 6 5 4 3 2 1   ❖   First Edition